By Air, Sea, and Land
Special Engines

Paul Stickland

WATERBIRD BOOKS
Columbus, Ohio

Moving Van

This is a **moving van**.

Furniture is loaded into it and taken to a home.

More About Moving Vans

Moving vans are packed full of furniture and other belongings to be moved from one place to another. The movers use the back door as a ramp to carry the furniture into the van.

Moving vans are so big that they need extra large mirrors on each side. This helps the driver can see around the van.

Ambulance

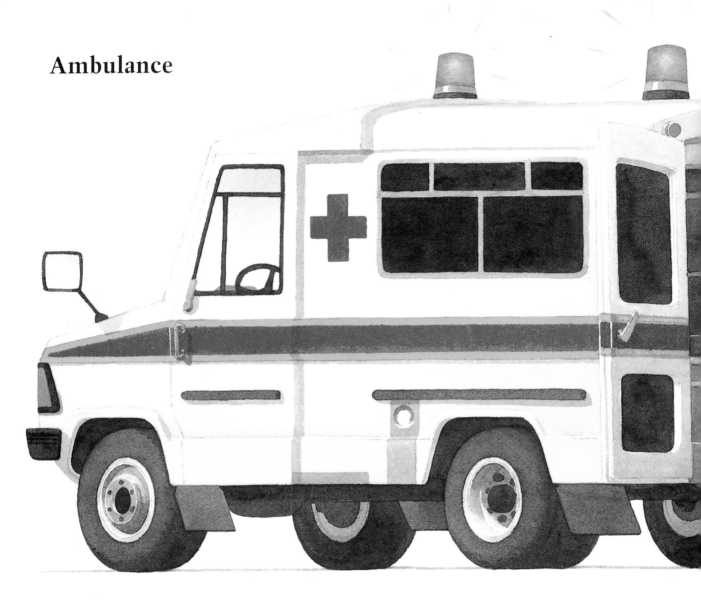

Ambulances are used to transport sick or hurt people to the hospital.

More About Ambulances

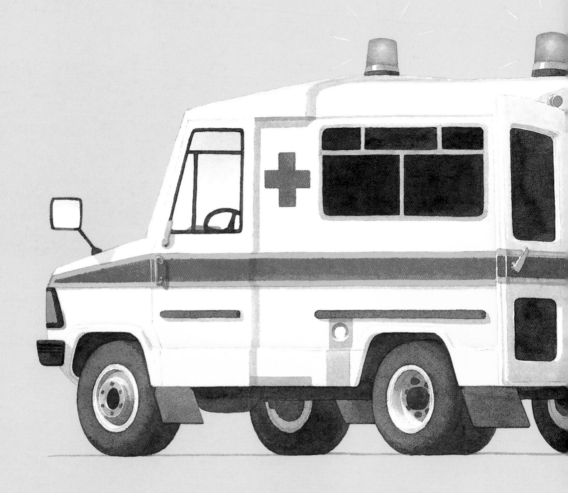

Ambulances are allowed to drive through red lights and break the speed limit so they can get their patients to the hospital quickly. They have flashing lights that warn other drivers that they are coming.

Ambulance crews are medically trained so that they can help their patients. The ambulance is stocked with bandages, medicines, and emergency equipment.

Street Sweeper

Street sweepers keep the street clean.

Cement Mixer

A **cement mixer** transports and pours concrete.

More About Street Sweepers

Street sweepers have brushes that move trash from the gutter and toward the vacuum pipe. Then, the big vacuum sucks the garbage up into the storage tank.

More About Cement Mixers

Cement mixers deliver concrete to construction sites. The barrel turns, keeping the concrete from becoming hard. A slide, called a *chute*, directs the cement to the pouring site.

Fire Engine

Fire engines are used by firefighters to fight fires.

More About Fire Engines

Fire engines have everything that firefighters need to fight fires, like hoses, searchlights, and safety equipment.

This fire engine has a crane that carries the firefighter high in the air. The firefighter can spray water on the fire from above.

Steamroller

Steamrollers are used to make a new road smooth and flat.

More About Steamrollers

A steamroller has to be as heavy as possible so that it can flatten the road. These machines are very slow. Steamrollers have scrapers to keep stones from sticking to the wheels.

The steamroller crushes and rolls the stones to make a flat surface. Then, the worker spreads the asphalt. The steamroller rolls the asphalt until it is flat.

What Did You Learn?

What does this truck carry?

Is this truck used
inside or outside?

How can you tell that this is a
snow removal truck?

How can you tell that this is a police car?

What is this worker doing?

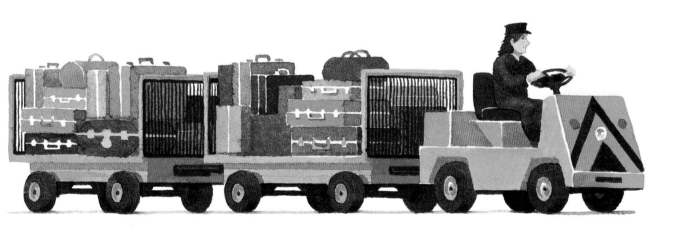

Where is this trailer going?

This is a garbage truck. It collects trash and carries it to the garbage dump.

You can tell this is a police car by its flashing light and the police inside the car.

This truck carries materials from place to place inside a warehouse.

The worker on the platform is replacing a bulb on a streetlight.

This truck is ready to clear snow with its blade and sprinkle salt on it.

This trailer is at an airport. It is taking luggage from the airport to the plane.

School Specialty
Children's Publishing

Copyright © Paul Stickland 1992, 2004
Designed by Douglas Martin.

This edition published in the United States of America in 2004
by Waterbird Books,
an imprint of School Specialty Children's Publishing,
a member of the School Specialty Family.
8720 Orion Place, Columbus, OH 43240-2111
www.ChildrensSpecialty.com

Library of Congress Cataloging-in-Publication is on file with the publisher.

ISBN 0-7696-3376-5
Printed in China.

1 2 3 4 5 6 7 8 MP 08 07 06 05 04